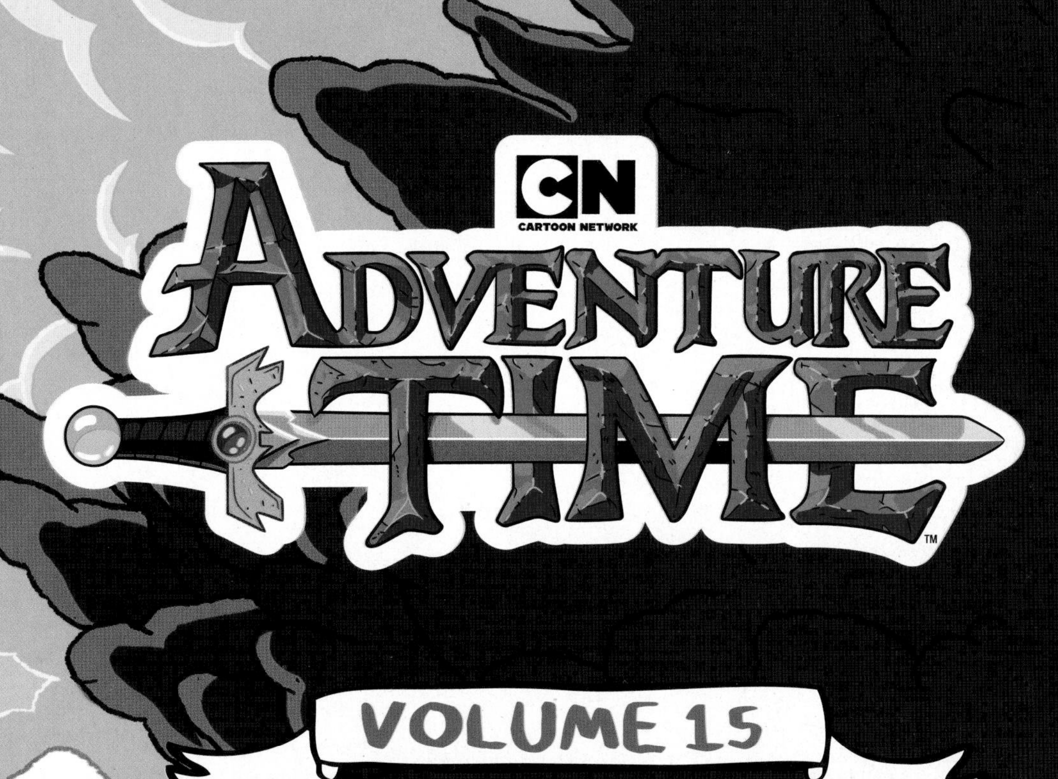
CN
CARTOON NETWORK
ADVENTURE
TIME
VOLUME 15

ADVENTURE TIME Volume Fifteen, August 2018. Published by KaBOOM!, a division of Boom Entertainment, Inc.

For information regarding the CPSIA on this printed material, call (203) 595-3636 and provide reference #RICH - 785216.

BOOM! Studios, 5670 Wilshire Boulevard, Suite 400, Los Angeles, CA 90036-5679. Printed in USA. First Printing.

ISBN: 978-1-68415-203-2, eISBN: 978-1-64144-018-9

CREATED BY
Pendleton Ward

WRITTEN BY
Delilah S. Dawson

ILLUSTRATED BY
Ian McGinty

COLORS BY
Maarta Laiho

LETTERS BY
Mike Fiorentino

COVER BY
Shelli Paroline & Braden Lamb

DESIGNER
Jillian Crab

ASSISTANT EDITOR
Michael Moccio

EDITOR
Whitney Leopard

With Special Thanks to Marisa Marionakis, Janet No, Curtis Lelash, Conrad Montgomery, Kelly Crews, Scott Malchus, Adam Muto and the wonderful folks at Cartoon Network.

Special delivery for the princess!
And spa day goes kerplop.
I remember when this jazz used to be exciting.

Princess!
Princess Bubblegum's boring room for doing totally normal things during secret quiet time.
STAY
This is my secret quiet time when I'm doing totally normal things, remember?

My lady, you have an important visitor bearing gifts.
It is my solemn vow as your butler to buttle.
And I do not forsake my vows.
Gifts? What kind of gifts?

Alright, let's see what's worth interrupting my sacred rit--
Epsom salt bath.

Your majesty, I present Stanley Nougat.
Stanley Nougat? I don't recognize you.
Are you from the Breakfast Kingdom?
Er, yes. But I travel a lot.
Hoo golly, did I have some fun doing adventures and stuff.
That's where I found this.
Ooo!
What is it, highness?

I'm only going to explain it once, Pep.
Let's see. Bring me Finn, Jake, LSP, and Marceline.
Chop chop! Get that butt butlering!

Because I'm gonna kick everybody's keister.

Hey, man. Do you ever wonder why we exist?
Pssh. No way, bro times. I'm just a sheep. Doing sheepy things.
You start thinking about stuff like that, and you'll stay up all night just thinking about stuff.
That's what it's like, getting old, dude. Like, a lot of feelings are involved.
Also, your ears will grow, like, a ton of hair.
No time for feelings, Finn and Jake. The Princess sends an invitation!
Uh, I had feelings once. Then I stopped having them. It's easier, now.
BA-BA-BA-BALLOOON RACE!
Finn and Jake,
You are hereby invited to join me for a HOT AIR BALLOOON RACE.
That is, a ballooon race around Ooo. No joke. Totes for real. For real real. Meet me at the Royal Ballooon Grounds at dawn.
Did they say baa?
Ignore them. They know nothing of our ways.

Wait, guys! There's a P.S.!

P.S. THERE'S A PRIZE!

A PRIZE?!?!

Yes, there's a prize! You guys should read the whole thing before you react!
Now I've got to go deliver the other invitations.

Hmm... other invitations?
Good point. We're gonna beat the SHMOWZOW out of 'em! Whoever they are.
Bro times, there's got to be other people in the race.
Otherwise, who would we beat to win THE PRIZE?
But first, it's...

Time to pack!

What do we even pack for a ballooon race?

I guess we need to plan for anything.
Like, the thing that saves us could be the thing we didn't think we needed.

Finn and Jake! You made a big mess. This is not coolio.
You need to pack underpants and sweaters!

And you also need to pack your pal BMO!
I guess BMO's right. Tootsies are gonna get frosty, up there.
And it's always better to be toasty than frozety!
Frozety is not a word.

Hi, guys! Are you ready to race?
I will be. Soonish. I was up all night packing. What's the dealio, anyways?
Dealio, schmealio. Wake me up when we're afloat, yo.
Don't leave me snoring and do it solo.
You didn't need to pack anything, silly!
I've supplied everything you need in this trunk.
DUMP

OH MY GOSH, BRO.
IT'S ADVENTURING TOGS!

Now here's the dealio.

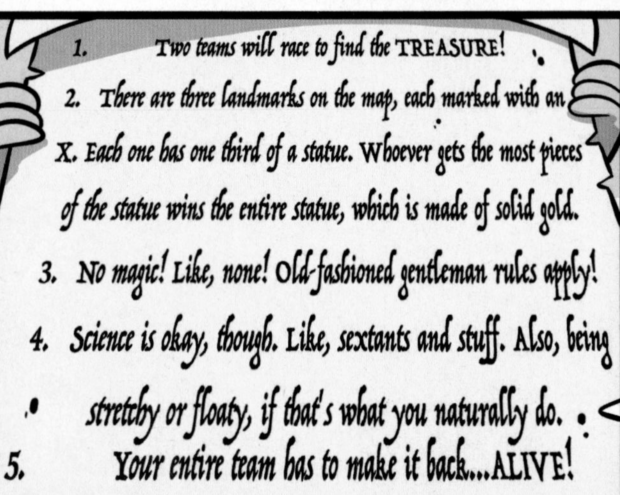
1. Two teams will race to find the TREASURE!
2. There are three landmarks on the map, each marked with an X. Each one has one third of a statue. Whoever gets the most pieces of the statue wins the entire statue, which is made of solid gold.
3. No magic! Like, none! Old-fashioned gentleman rules apply!
4. Science is okay, though. Like, sextants and stuff. Also, being stretchy or floaty, if that's what you naturally do.
5. Your entire team has to make it back...ALIVE!

Uh, Pubbles? Where did you get this jazz?
It seems, like, oddly specific to our friends.
Even though it looks old and moldy, it doesn't sound old and moldy.
Yeah, there's not a single YE or OLDE or the word SHOPPE.

Where's your sense of adventure?
Are you really worried something's up...
...or are you afraid of looooooosing?
She's right. I'm in. WE AIN'T GONNA LOSE! YOU IS!
I still have some questions. Like why are there only two teams?

Because of fractions! There are three parts of the statue and three locations, which means that if there were more than two teams--
Ugh. Too mathematical. Let's just go.

Boys, this is Stanley Nougat.
He's an adventurer and cartographer*, and he's the final member of your team.
He's going to make sure your ballooon stays on course.
Whaaaaaat? Who's this guy?
Right? I feel unusually hostile toward outsiders. I think it's the helmet.
But if he's a candy peep, he's got to be cool. Cuz Peebs made him, right?

Hey, there... you.
What's up, Stanley the Candymanly?
Um. Balloons are up, my chum.
R
Greetings!
Turtle Princess here. As the official race reporter, I'm bringing you exciting...word definitions!
*Cartographer (noun): Someone who draws maps. Very different from a fartographer.

And the teams are...
VS
Finn! Put down the sword, silly! It's a race, not a...ham slicing contest.
I'm so excited!

* Aviatrix (noun): A lady pilot. Not a bird. Just sayin'.

Side note: Wind is never to be taken lightly.

*Sextant (noun): A navigation instrument that measures the angle between two visible objects. So, like, a thing for maps.

*Defenestrate (verb): To throw out of a window. In this case, it's a ballooon but there's not a word for that. Deballooonestrating just sounds weird.

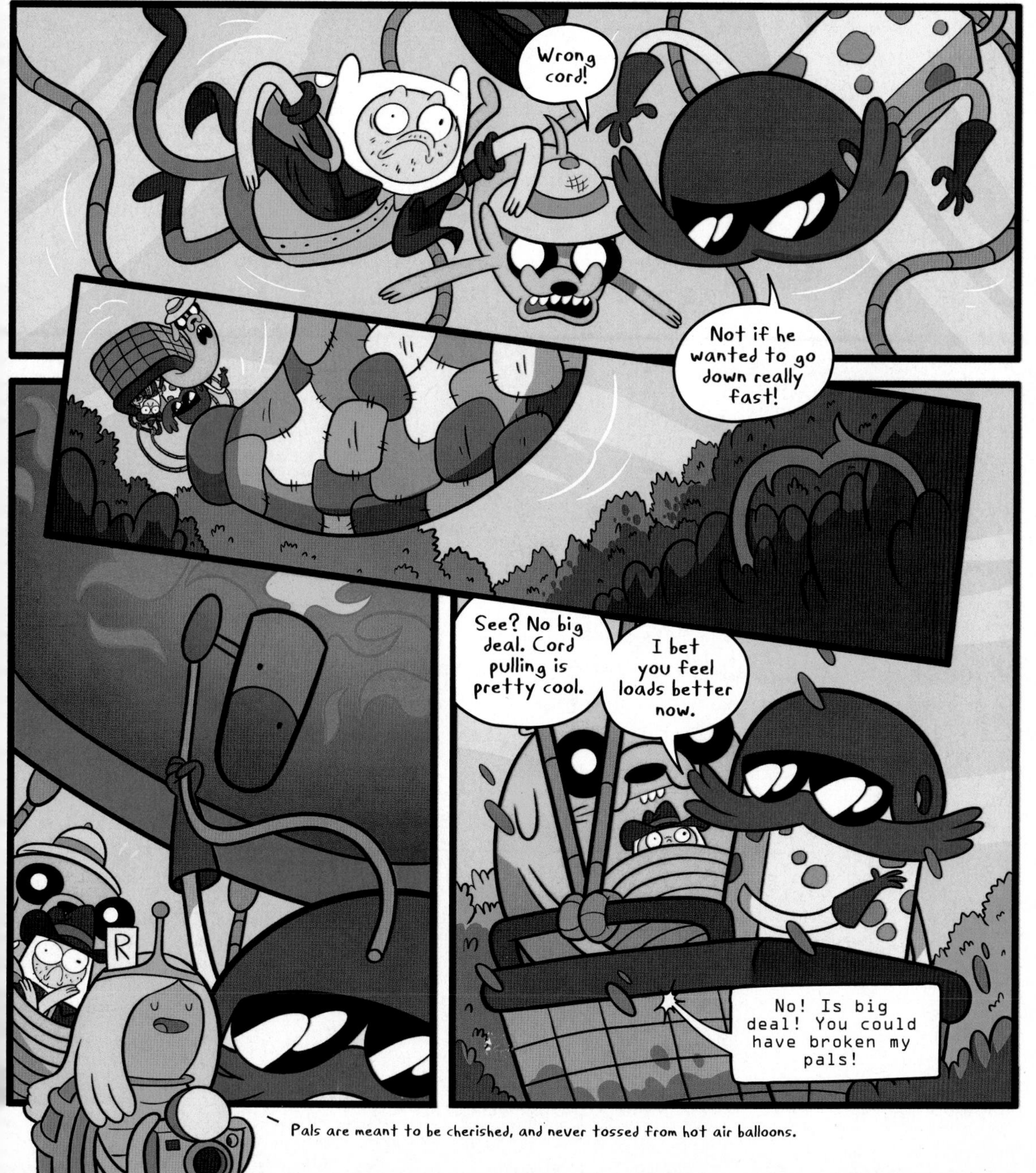

Pals are meant to be cherished, and never tossed from hot air balloons.

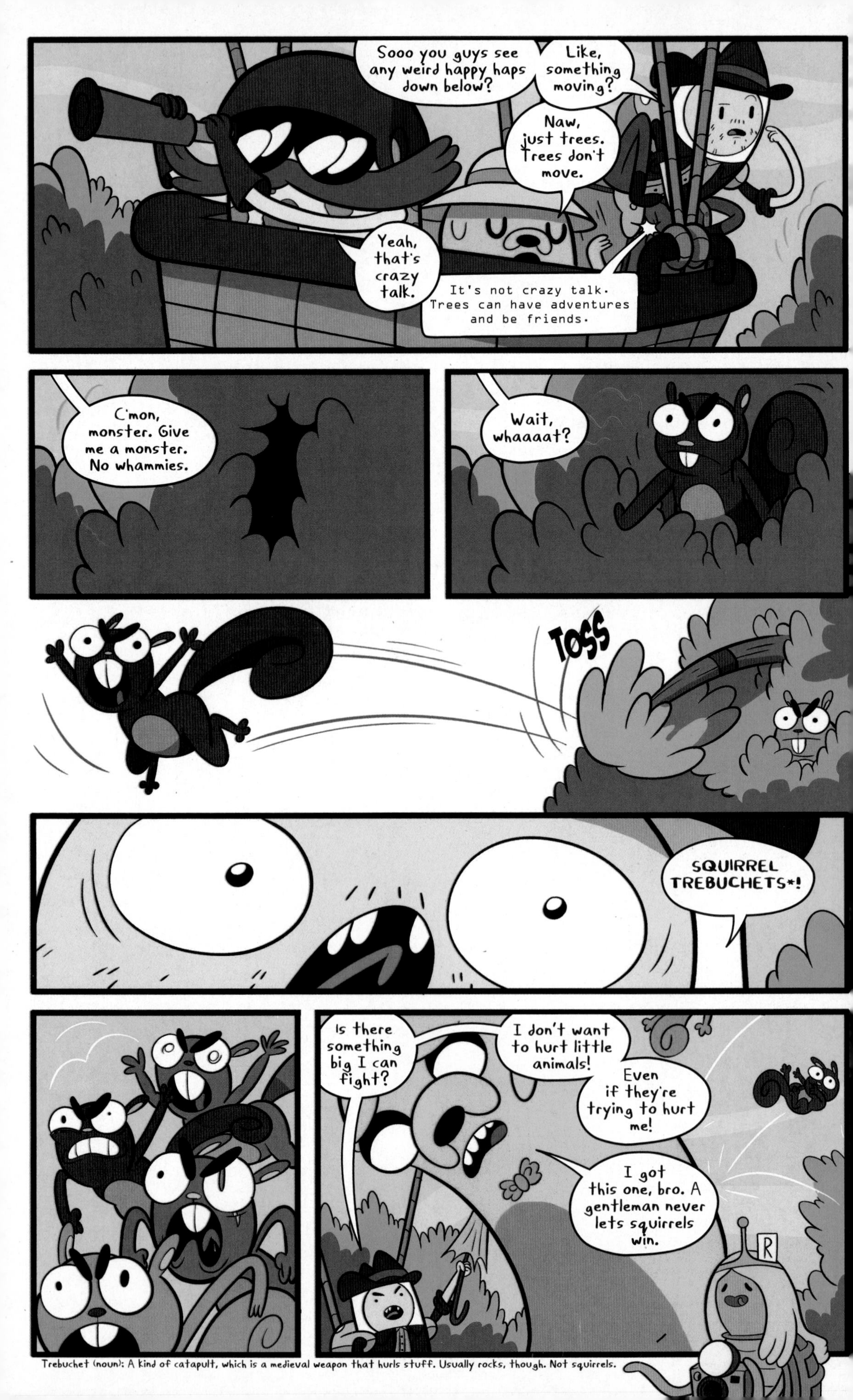

Trebuchet (noun): A kind of catapult, which is a medieval weapon that hurls stuff. Usually rocks, though. Not squirrels.

*Absquatulate (verb): To flee, to abscond, to leave abruptly.

*Pedant (noun): a person who is excessively concerned with minor details and rules or with displaying academic learning.

*Fantabulator (Noun): That thing PB said. Okay, so fantabulator isn't actually a word, but it should be. Language is fluid.

*Fisticuffs (noun): Boxing. Like, fighting with your fists. But you already knew that, right, champ?

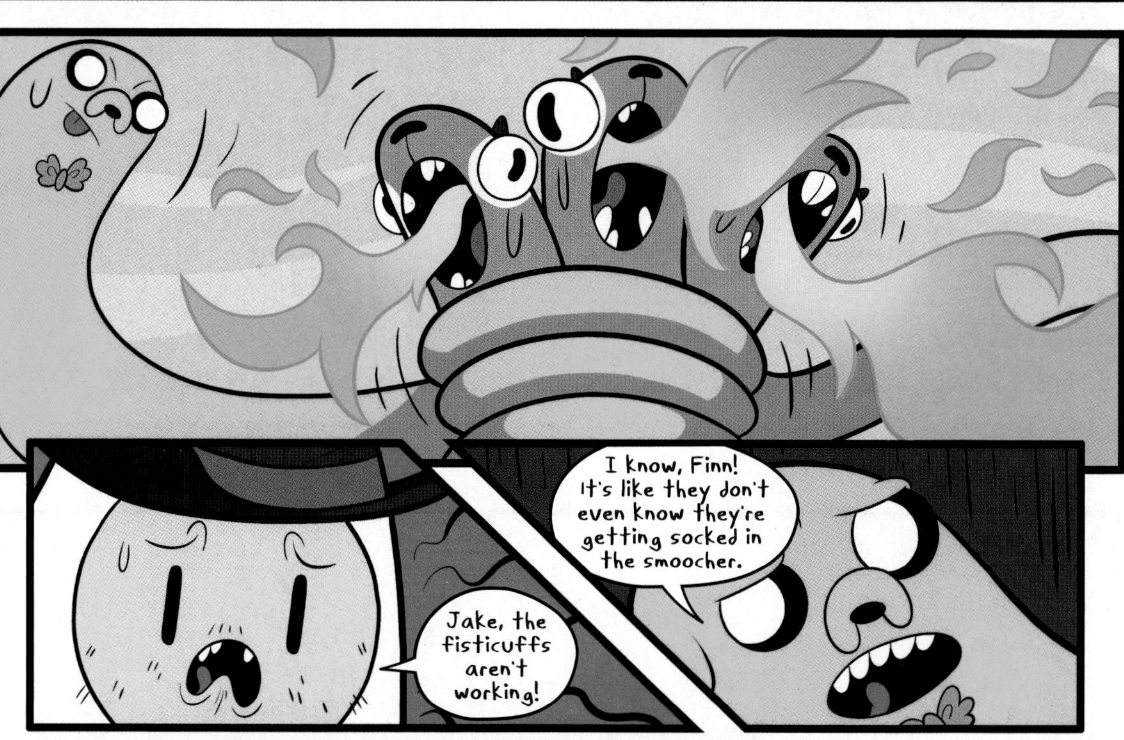

*Ziggurat (noun): An ancient Mesopotamian temple tower. Kinda like a pyramid.

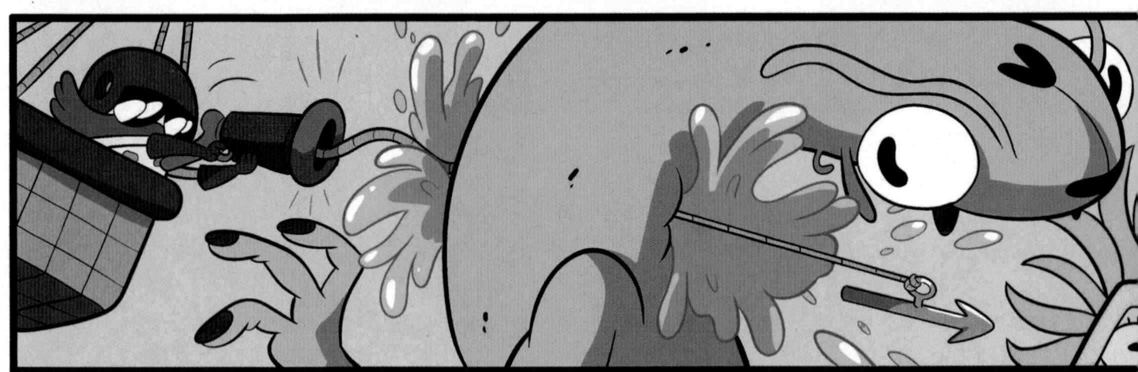

Real deer can't breathe fire...and typically aren't made out of avocados.

*Immolate (verb): To kill or destroy by fire. Very different from **EMULATE**. Just sayin'.

*Phantasmagoric (adjective): Dreamy, weird, changing, shifting. Gee, where have we seen that before?

Jake, I've got a feeling we're not in our regular place anymore, yo!

What happened?
I think that was a cyclone, bro.
It was a tornado, which is a violently rotating column of air that--
I'm so tired of air.
Is everyone alright?
Can somebody be a chum and help ol' Stanley Nougat up?
I'm a bit bumfuzzled*.
I'm back with more funcabulary! Which is fun vocabulary. But that's not the word for this page, which is BUMFUZZLED (adjective): Confused.

O pulchritudinous* one, you have squished the Evil Earl of the East.
We are finally free!
Uh, okay.
Aw! Cute King! You're still not large and in charge!
I am no longer in charge!
The Earl of the East stole my crown.
Now whoever murdled--I MEAN, ACCIDENTALLY SQUISHED--him is king.
I got enough trubs. I need to get these balloons up again so I can win this race.
You can keep your crown.
BMO vanquished this varlet! All hail King BMO!
And BMO looks so boy-howdy in the squished person's fancy shoes!
*PULCHRITUDINOUS (adjective): Physically beautiful. But it sounds gross, which makes it FUN.

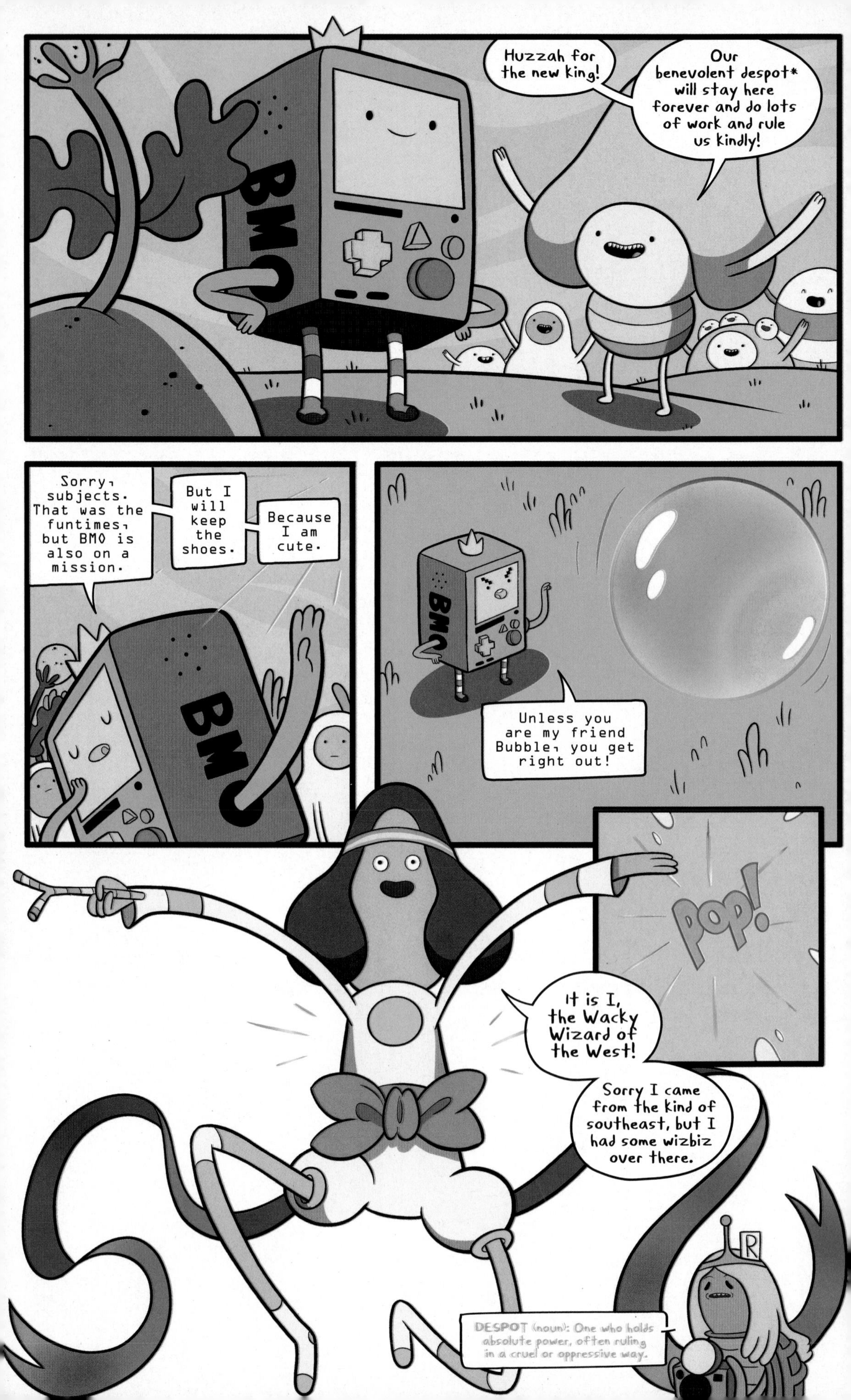
Huzzah for the new king!
Our benevolent despot* will stay here forever and do lots of work and rule us kindly!
Sorry, subjects. That was the funtimes, but BMO is also on a mission.
But I will keep the shoes.
Because I am cute.
Unless you are my friend Bubble, you get right out!
POP!
It is I, the Wacky Wizard of the West!
Sorry I came from the kind of southeast, but I had some wizbiz over there.
DESPOT (noun): One who holds absolute power, often ruling in a cruel or oppressive way.

COLLYWOBBLES (noun): Stomach pain or queasiness, often caused by anxiety. Also known as a thing adults experience pretty much every moment.

AW, YEAH, ADVENTURE!
Need to stretch these muscles!
...if we must.
Hey, where's Marceline?
I have developed an army and am ready to annex something!

I'm back, yo!
Here's the sewing kit. I just walked, like, really fast and got it.
That Wizard of Oooze is gross.
You didn't walk, like, really fast! You used magic!
You can't prove that.
Fine. Hand over the thread.
Let's just get out of here before somebody worse shows up.
Gosh, you guys. I thought I could be like your guide.
But I guess you don't need me anymore.
I abdicate*.
But I'm keeping the shoes.
It is for the best.
I would've fiddled while Oooze burned.
Just stay away from my viola!
ABDICATE (verb): To renounce one's throne. And not as in toilet.

This is the least adventuresome adventure ever.
I mean, if Abracadorkel is the king, this place is badonkers boring.
HEY, OOOZE! SEND ME A BAD GUY TO FIGHT OR I'LL PUNCH YOU IN A STUMP!

I wouldn't expect a younger person to know this, but asking for trouble when things are chill is generally uncool.

Youth culture rules!

5 Seconds Later.
Never mind! Let's go!

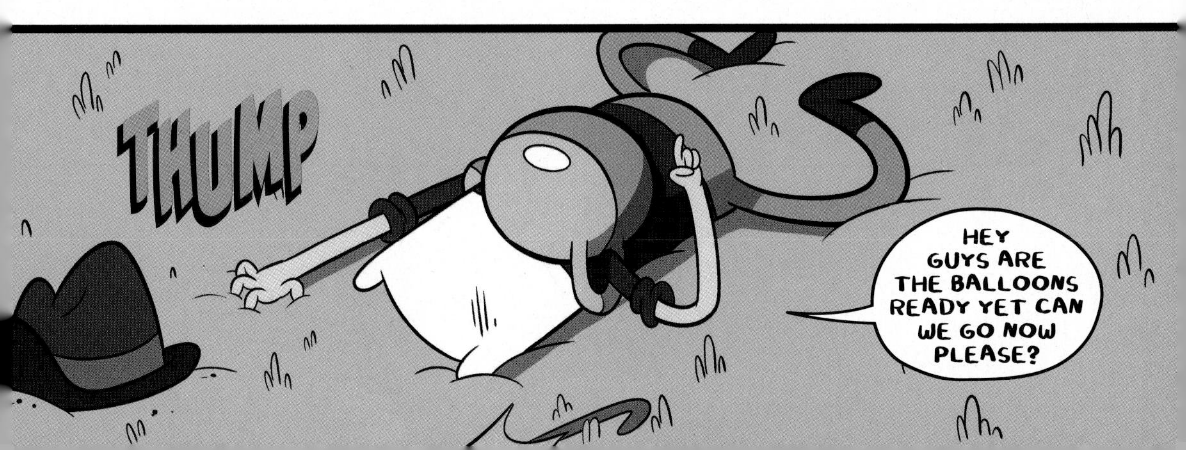
THUMP
HEY GUYS ARE THE BALLOONS READY YET CAN WE GO NOW PLEASE?

So, you guys. Um. How do you feel about angry monkeyflies?
Are they good? Do you feel good about them?
Oh, and it looks like their leader is a winged battle hippo, so that's interesting, right?
Like, nature?
You poked their hive, didn't you?
I did. I poked their hive.
But I didn't know it was a hive! It looked fun!
But I can't let them poke us back.
SORRY ABOUT THIS!
Wait for me, bro!
Uh, Marcy? We may need you. And your floatin'.

Sorry!
POW

Just go back, I won't bother you again!
WHACK!!
Is there anything this weirdo won't fight?
He's truly rude, crude, and socially unacceptable.

Now would be a good time to get huge or bouncy, bro.
Nah. I made arrangements.

How's about a little deus ex Marceline, boys?

Get ready. We're about to get outta here!

Ploop!
Thanks, Marceline!
Again with the magic! You have no respect for rules!
Not really. Bye!
She is like a wild stallion that cannot be roped.

You need to chill, Stanman.
We're on a journey.
BMO

No way! That's a childish way to look at it.
Rules matter. Cheating cheapens your journey.
Don't you care about who you are when no one is looking?

I mean, I think we know who we are.
Yeah! I know who I am!
I also know who I am...I think.

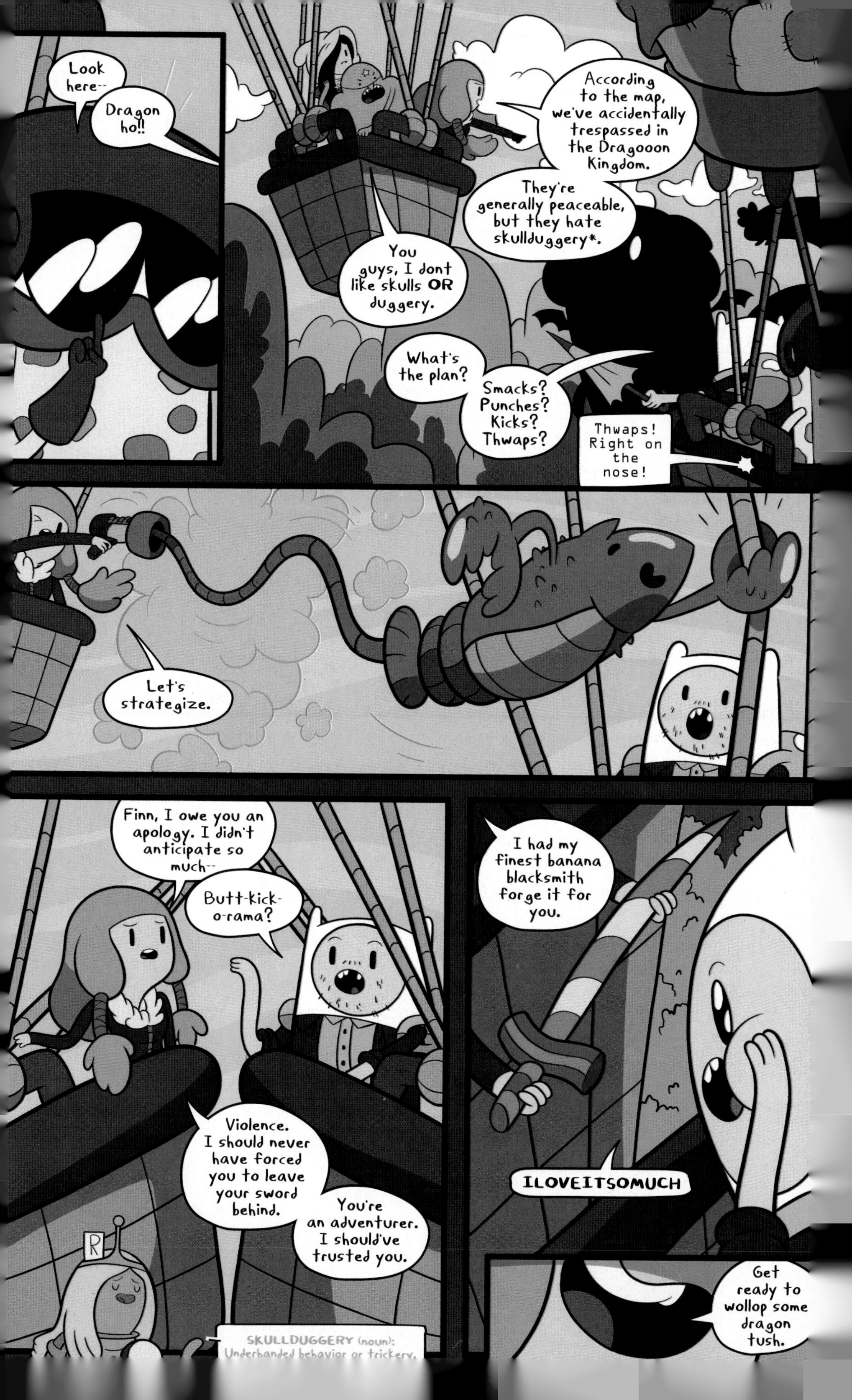
Look here--
Dragon ho!!
According to the map, we've accidentally trespassed in the Dragooon Kingdom.
They're generally peaceable, but they hate skullduggery*.
You guys, I dont like skulls OR duggery.
What's the plan?
Smacks? Punches? Kicks? Thwaps?
Thwaps! Right on the nose!
Let's strategize.
Finn, I owe you an apology. I didn't anticipate so much--
Butt-kick-o-rama?
Violence. I should never have forced you to leave your sword behind.
You're an adventurer. I should've trusted you.
I had my finest banana blacksmith forge it for you.
ILOVEITSOMUCH
Get ready to wollop some dragon tush.
SKULLDUGGERY (noun): Underhanded behavior or trickery.

DRAGON, ARE YOU READY FOR SOME GOOD OL' SNICKERSNEE*?

Do you mean fighting?
Yeah, I mean fighting!
Then no. Definitely not.
Not IS an option, right?

Yeah, not fighting is always an option.
As long as you're cool with us floating through your biz.

It's not my biz. Nobody owns the air.
Just, please...NO SKULLDUGGERY.

That's cool, but a bit of a downer.
I bet there'll be some crazy bad boss when we get to the next statue, at least.
R
SNICKERSNEE (noun): Fighting that involves knives or blades. Isn't it fun to say?

Are we supposed to go inside that crazy complex?
And fight stuff?
Probably. The statues are just Xs on my map.
And, you know, I've got that crazy wizard vision.
Wait, what?
I said hazy blizzard fiction. Um, I write it.
When I'm not adventuring, I'm a novelist.
I can't believe my fantabulator was destroyed in the tornado.
It doesn't matter, Bonnie. It messed us up last time.
This time, we'll be the ones on the other side.
Yeah, you guys go ahead. I'll, like, guard the balloon.
I don't like small, dark, creepy places full of spiders.
WAIT!! I DON'T WANT TO BE ALONE EITHER!

TRIP

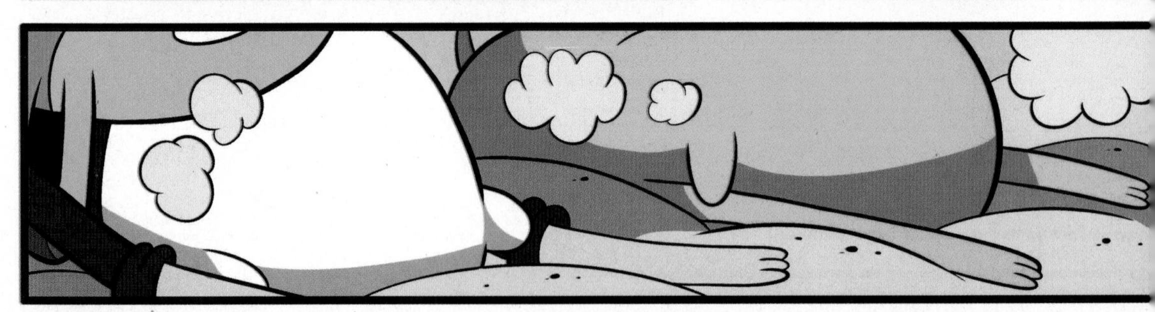

Spiders. Why's it always gotta be spiders?

So magic is borked but tripping is okay?
Those rules are totes not cool.
There's nothing against trippage, sadly.
Right? Jakey don't like eatin' sand!

Uh, PB? Did you bring a light? Because... science?

PHOSPHORESCENT (adj.): Enduring luminescence without heat. So, light without fire. Also involves radiation. But don't worry about that. PB said it was safe, and she would never lie.

NO! I'm too beautiful to end this way!
It's a mummy. Not that scary.

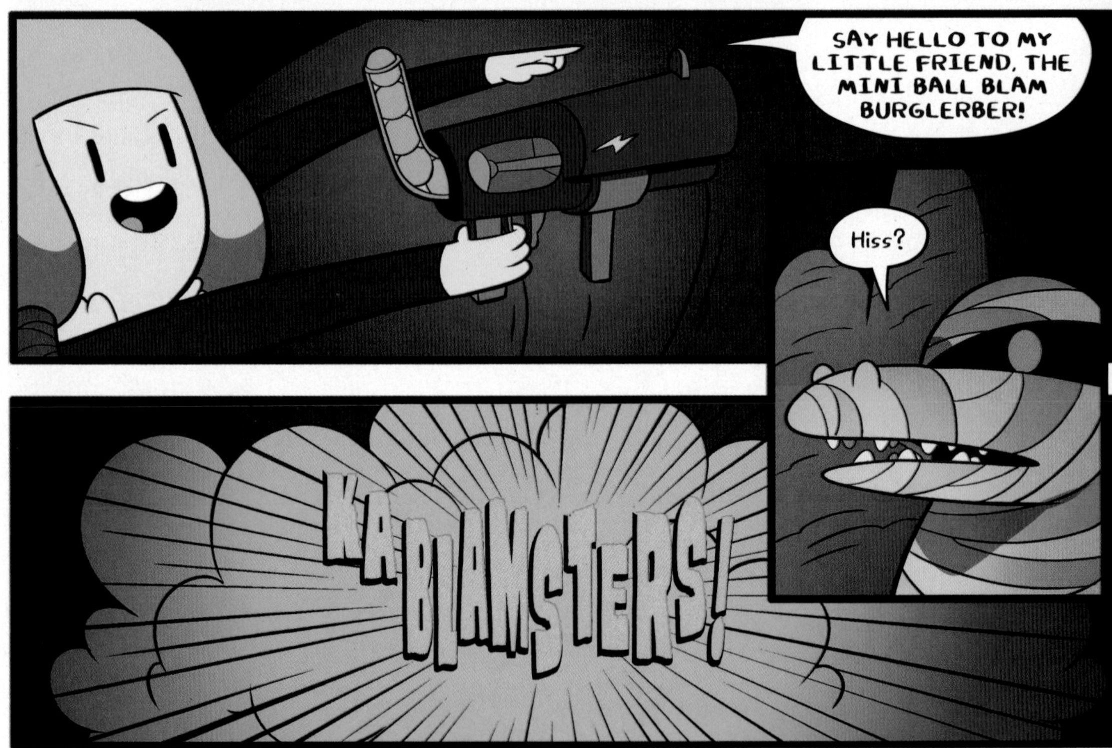
SAY HELLO TO MY LITTLE FRIEND, THE MINI BALL BLAM BURGLERBER!
Hiss?
KA-BLAMSTERS!

Whoa dang. You totally decimated* that mummycroc.
If you've had that thing with you all along, why is this the first time you've used it?
I'm a wait-and-see, last resort kind of girl.
Besides, it makes Finn and Jake happy to fight things.
R
DECIMATE (verb): To reduce by 10%. So PB decimated the mummycroc, like, 10 times.

Floating sideways is not good for my lumps, you guys.
I'm gonna be lumpin' lopsided!
Why are you even climbing?
We can totes float you up. Right, Marcy?
I feel kinda bad for tripping the guys now.
They would love this place.
Whatevs. You snooze you lose.
I know what you mean. Finn would flip.
Well, I haven't lost my zest for jeopardy*.
I'm doing it. And no magic this time.
Can you hold this, Peebs?
JEOPARDY (noun): Exposure to danger.

WHOOSH!
Something about this just feels wrong.
It's like deja vu, but bad.
Heh. Deja EWWW.
I got it, yo!
CREEEAK!
Uh oh. The bat's out of the belfry*, babies.
We gotta get outtie.
BELFRY (noun): A siege tower, or 'that which watches over the peace'. Also, a place where bats loooove to party. Words are weird.

Snakes and **SPIDERS?!** Nope.

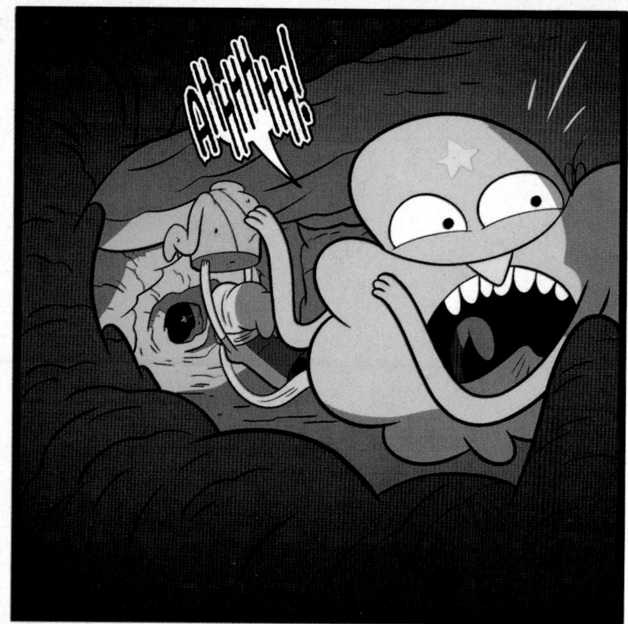

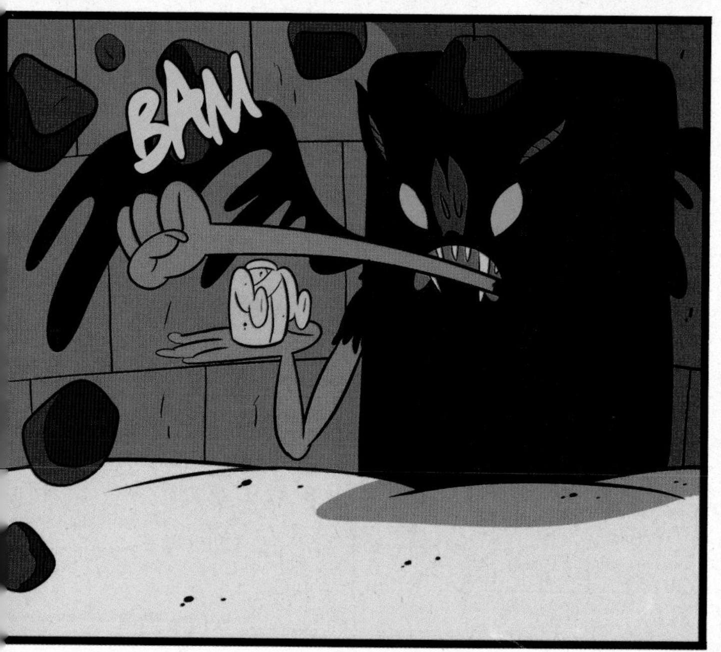
BAM

Hey Peebs, you didn't lose my hat, did you?
Well... about that...

CHIVALRY (noun): A knightly code of conduct. Fun fact: It was originally about horse ownership and had nothing to do with being a nice guy.

They greased it! With sea lard grease!
Oh, nasty.
This is so not okay.

It's kinda funny, though. I tripped them, they slipped you.
Now you're all nizasty.
And you smell like pickles mixed with slugs.
You should look after those lumps, girl.
I have an idea. And it's not cheating. TECHNICALLY.
But you guys have to do what I say.

LSP, can you sing your lumps song?

And LSP, I need you to dance.
We need to party.
And I mean HEARTY.

WOW, WHAT A GREAT PARTY!
I KNOW, RIGHT? THIS IS THE BEST PARTY I'VE EVER BEEN TO.
C'mon, c'mon, c'mon...
Did somebody say PARTY?

Woohoo!
I'm glad to help, but they're kinda waiting for me back at the party pad.
I was supposed to bring hot dog buns and be back in ten.

Turtle Princess is back with the rad vocab! Just remember: **STALACTITES** point down, and **STALAGMITES** point up.

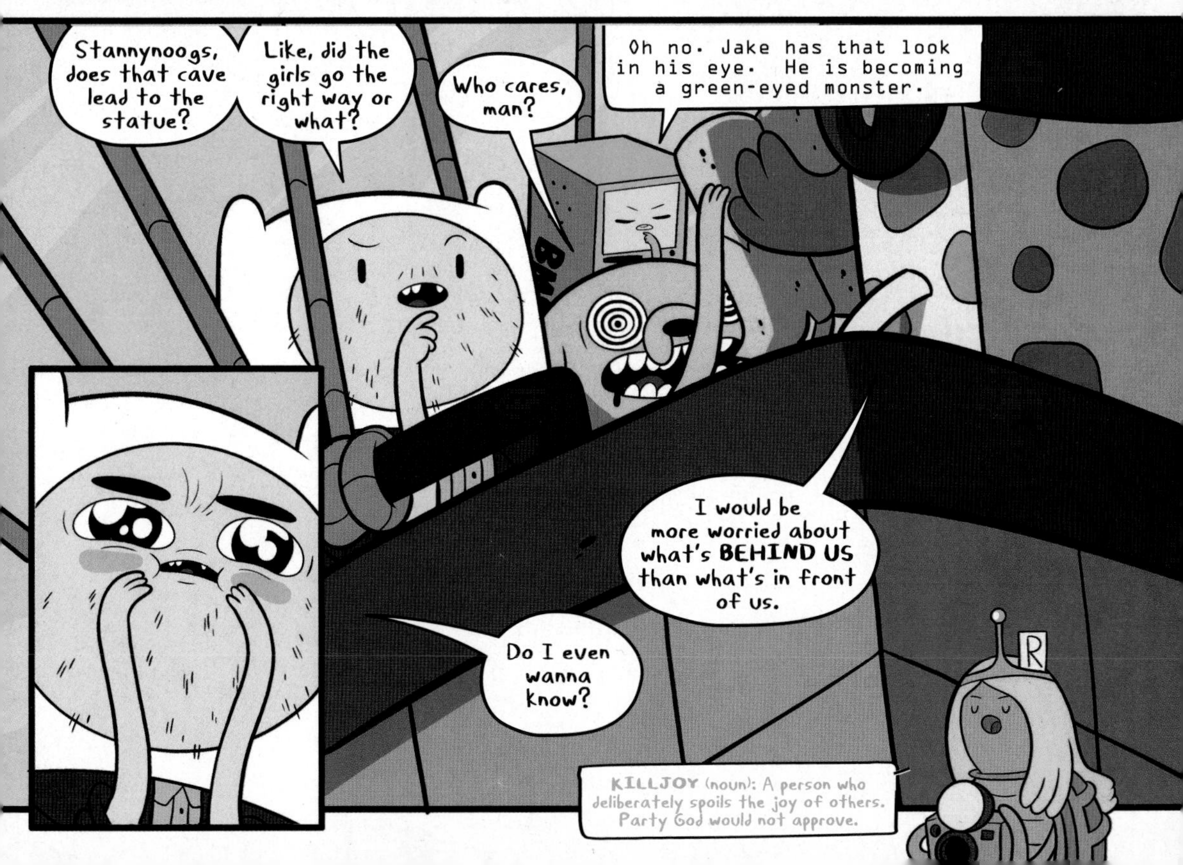

KILLJOY (noun): A person who deliberately spoils the joy of others. Party God would not approve.

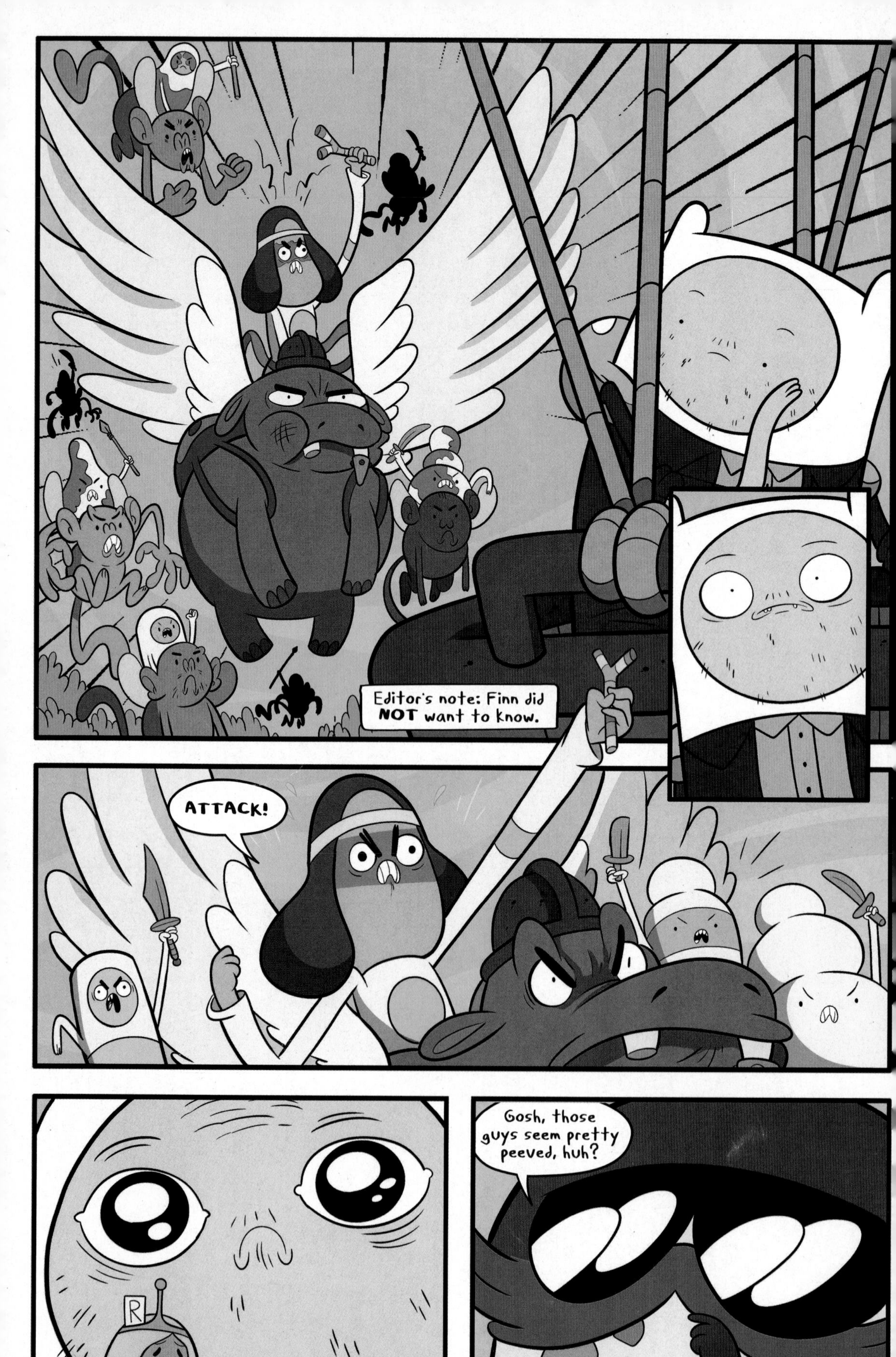
Editor's note: Finn did NOT want to know.
ATTACK!
Gosh, those guys seem pretty peeved, huh?
R
There are only 16 words on this page, so here's a FUN FLY FACT: Flies can't chew. Also, they taste with their feet.

What are we going to do?
Remember? How the last fight with these guys didn't go so swell?
KISS KISS
Just look at it, man.
Just... feet. So great.
KISS KISS
Stanley! Please tell me you're a kung fu master!
Do not. Touch. THE STACHE.
But, yes, I do have a very particular set of skills.
Skills that I have acquired over--
NOT THE BEST TIME TO BOMBINATE*, BRO.
R
BOMBINATE (verb): To make a buzzing noise or deep, hollow sound.
So at this point, it's probably half Stannynoogs and half angry monkeyfly.

...

DO YOUR THANG, STANNYNOOGS!

Oh. Okay. Now? Like, right now?
YES, RIGHT NOW.
Then turn around. I'm kinda shy about my skillz.

Ooookay. Here we go.
This is totally normal and in no way against the rules, just FYI.

OH LOOK. IT'S SUDDEN, RANDOM WEATHER. HOW USEFUL.

VELOCIOUS (adjective): Speedy or fast. Which is different from a **VELOCIPEDE**, which is a tricycle.

Yeah, and this isn't magic, either.
If what Stanley did is icing, I guess this is i-stretching.
All according to plan.

Huh. Standard cave. Creepy bats.
Maybe there's something to fight inside!
Hm. Look! Butterbats. You can tell by the mounds of margarine on the ground.
It's probably pretty boring here if there's butterbats.

Oh boy! Is time for spelunking*! I will light the way.
Sure wish I had my sword. Or that ol' umbrella. Or anything weapony.

Don't worry, buddy. We'll be fine. Won't we?
Who said that?
...you're talking to the statue, aren't you?
Finn, you are now my girl, who I shall call Friday.
Take a memo, Friday: The cave is getting weird.

Whoa! Why are there clocks? You think I'm gonna get **CLOCKED**, BMO?
It is a cave, not a book of puns, Friday.
SPELUNKING (verb): The practice of exploring caves.

OLEO (noun): An old-fashioned word for margarine, which is an old-fashioned word for "they used to think butter was bad for us." It's not. Butter is one of the seven food groups.

How rude. You should respect your elders.

Maybe you should do something worthy of respect then, Gramps!
What happened to you, Stanley? It get you too?
I dunno, man. I was just standing here, and I was suddenly infinitely COOLER.
I feel YOUNG AGAIN...But I can't remember who you're supposed to be. I thought you were supposed to forget stuff when you got OLDER not YOUNGER!

Being YOUNG doesn't make you COOL. It makes you ROWDY.
Being OLD doesn't make you WISE. It just means you're OVERSTAYING your welcome.
Finn, you are not being yourself. The time cave must've reversed your ages.
Those are very bad butterbats!
PURE BOY

That's what I think about being old!
Ouch! But I'm too tired to punch your buns.
PURE BOY
POOT

This is so messed up. I wonder why I'm not old or young?
You are a dog. Both old and young. Simultaneously eight and fifty-six.
See? SO MESSED UP.

Sure, it's messed up. But how do we fix it?
I dunno, man. I'm okay with it. Nothing hurts! My bunions* are gone!! Being young is **GREAT!**
PURE BOY

No, Stanley! We will fix this problem and get things back the way they should be!
I like things to stay the same. It's easier that way.

No way! #TeamNoBunions4eva!

Wait. What if he gets the statue first? We need to hurry!
Hurry? Gosh, no! That's the opposite of what to do.
We need to spend a lot of time arguing about what to do next.

Yeah, I'm done with this time junk. We need that statue.
I just feel really, really strongly about that part.
Unhand me, young man! I still need to clean up that margarine!
...no.
R
BUNION (noun): A painful swelling on the first joint of the first toe. Trust me: You don't want them.

There's no way to know if this is the right way.
It smells like it's the wrong way. Unless it's the way to NASTYVILLE.
Yeah, Marcy's right. Why would anybody put gold somewhere so gross?

Oh, ick, you guys. It's getting worse.
Maybe that means we're getting closer? It does smell very scientific.
I hope the boys are okay.
Only you would think that smelling scientific was a good sign.
And the boys are fine. They're tough.

Well, that's as yuck as it smells.
C'mon. Let's go. Why are you guys being weird?
That's the river EGGETHON. It's made of the souls of rotten eggs.
It punishes those who have committed--
Yeah, I'm not crossing that.

You listen here. You dragged me on this dumb adventure, and I didn't want to go, but there were sammiches.
And now the sammiches are gone, and you're being wusses about crossing some gross river.
Well, I'm not a wuss. And there could be sammiches over there.

And now I'm going to get the statue and be the big cheese, so there!

Maybe there's another way around the aqueduct*.
She's going to need us if something really scary happens.
Stop acting like the **WORRY POLICE.** She's a grown...lumpy space person.
We just need to wait here and take care of the statue we've already got.
AQUEDUCT (noun): An artificial channel for water. But this is more like an eggquiduct.

YOU NEED TO CLEAN UP YOUR DIRTY BUTTER CAVE!
TIME CAVE 2: BUTTERBAT BOOGALOO
CLIFF OF INSANITY
Ho hum.
HALL OF SELF-HATRED
You guys are just jealous.
I am the apotheosis* of awesome.
I guess that's the statue, making me the winner.
Although why we care about some creepy old elf I don't even know.
APOTHEOSIS (noun): The highest point of the development of something. When I'm feeling down, I also stand in front of mirrors and remind myself that I'm the apotheosis of awesome. It works!

LITERALLY (adverb): In a literal sense, exactly. For example, if LSP said, "I am literally green with envy," she would be legally required to paint herself green. Or else. Being figuratively green with envy is allowed.

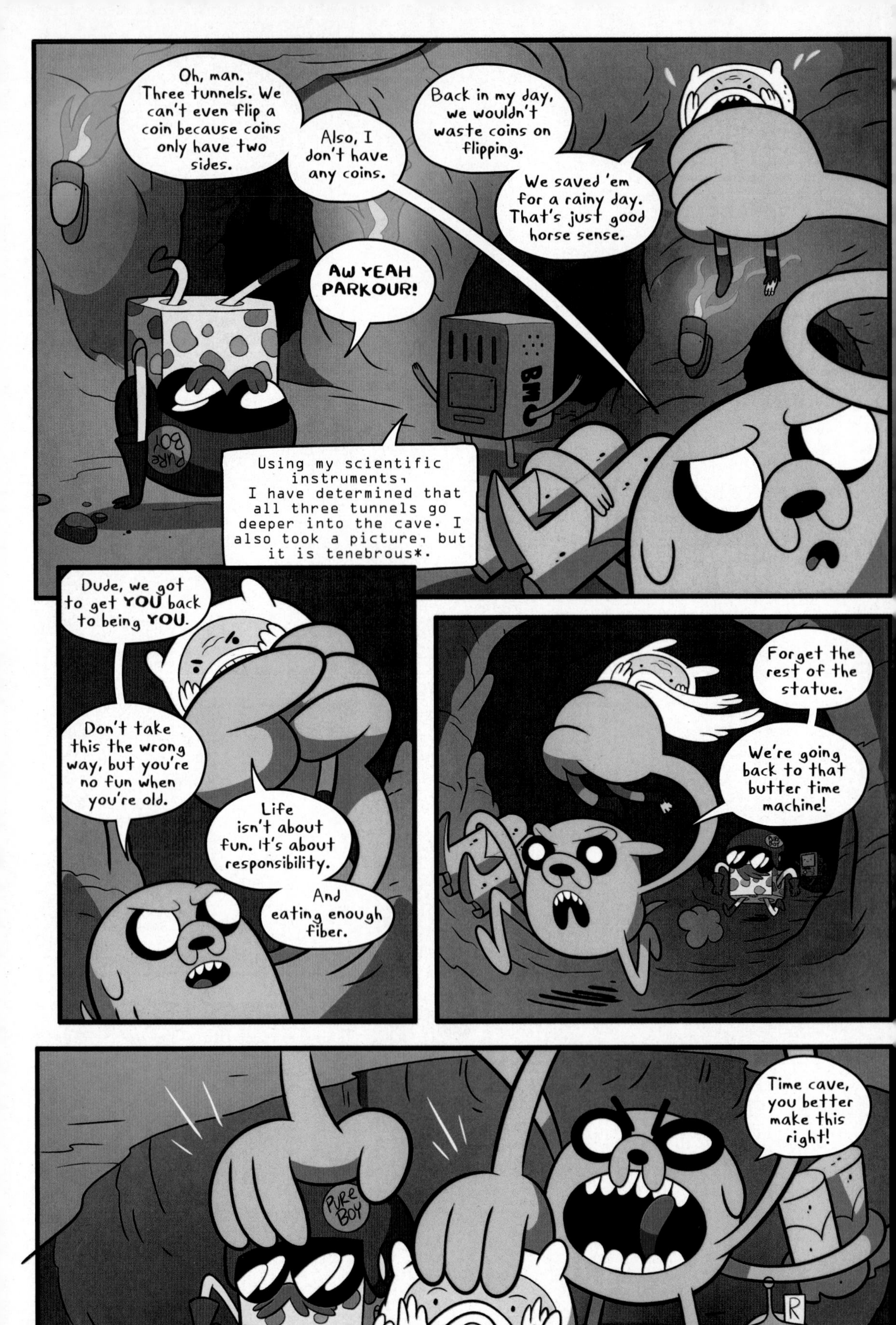

TENEBROUS (adjective): Full of darkness. Although that makes it sound less like the inside of a cave and more like a cup of coffee. Mmm. Coffee.

Okay, old buddy. How'd you donk up the time cave?
As a hasty youth, I carelessly smeared a line of margarine with my foot, an action I deeply regret.

Get ready to taste feet!

Well I never!
My youth!

It worked! You beat the butter! We're better than butter!
I know, dude! We battled bad butter and I ain't even bitter!
Well, actually, it's more like margarine.

Being old is the worst. Everything I had hurt.
Even my toenails. And I was craving tapioca* like crazy.
Mmm. Tapioca. With half a grapefruit. What a breakfast.

Now, let's go back to that fork and kick its tines!

I go left. Jake, you take the middle. Stanley and BMO, go right.
If there's trouble, scream.

This adventure is for bro times, not...hobbling down hallways alone.
I could do this at home.
Oooh, oooh, statue. You're so beautiful and feetly.
I wanna smooch your toesies.
YEAH COME ON I WANNA FIGHT MONSTERS WHAT
You are not alone. BMO is here! We are having B-times!
R
TAPIOCA (noun): A kind of pudding made from the roots of the cassava plant. It's basically ultra chunky health pudding, and old people go crazy for it. It's also what makes the bubbles in bubble tea.

JACKANAPES (noun): An impertinent person or a tame monkey, often used when describing a mischievous young boy. He doesn't have to be named Jack.

BEHEMOTH (noun): A huge and monstrous creature. Unrelated to moths. Unless it's a really big moth.

Jake, you can't just crush innocent people lumpin' down the hall.
Well you can't just stand underneath me when I'm fallin'.
Those lumps hurt!

The statue!

Whoopsy!

Well, well, well. What do you know?
Looks like the girls won!
Let's put this puppy together and gloat.
You were right, Peebs. Winning feels goood.
Aw! No! I got too attached.

Aw, man! Try again.
Uh, hold up. Stop. That looks like--
CLICK
Honey, I'm hooome!
This is the worst prize EVER!

Surprise!
Happy Deathday, Marceline!

DAD?! What is happening?
Why do you always have to embarrass me?
Embarrass you? Gosh, sweetie, I didn't mean to.
I'm just doin' mah hip Nightosphere dad thang, ya know?

This is almost worse than that time you wore bike shorts in public.

Hunson Abadeer, you evil so and so.
Are we doing this or what?
Yeah, it's time to punch some buns!

Bun-punching? No.
Punch and buns, yes!
After all, it's a Deathday party, not a fight.
This is how you guys party in Ooo, right? With fOood?

It's a... party?

It's a PARTY!!!
These lumps are ready to bump!
C'mon, everybody!
It's punch n' buns time!

Turtle Princess, what are you even doing here?
Shouldn't you be down at the bottom of the page?
I'm here for the party.
See? Here's my invite.
a Birthday Deathday Party!
For: Marceline
Date: after the Ballooon Race
Time: whenever you chuckleheads put the cursed statue together
Where: the Nightosphere
RSVP: Draw a happy face. Douse it with bug milk. Chant, "Maloso vobiscum et cum spiritum!" When the portal opens, leave a message.
Besides, ol' TP and I go way back.
We're the reigning Nightosphere Scrabble champions.
Go, Team Scrabble-cadabra!

Dad, can I talk to you in private?

Are you telling me that this whole balloon race was...
...an invitation to your surprise Deathday Party.
You never return my calls, so I had to get sneak-ay.
Want a party hat, sweetie?

NO, I DON'T WANT A PARTY HAT!
I TOLD YOU I DON'T LIKE DEATHDAY PARTIES.
AND I'M SURE MY FRIENDS HAD BETTER THINGS TO DO--

But honey-- They're your friends!
And your friends are having a nice time.
I thought you'd like it.

Is everything okay?
No, but I guess so?
This is not how I thought today was gonna go.
I know. I really, really wanted to win that race.
But your dad just loves you and wants to do nice things for you.
That's pretty normal for parents, I hear.

She's right, sweetie. I just want you to be happy.
And maybe a little evil.
Then you should have asked me what I wanted...

I think I finally get what you're saying, Marcy.
You do?
You want to play Pin the Tail on the Rotdragon!

You're still not listening to her.
How do you not get this?
I think I know what this is about.
She wants what every little girl wants, doesn't she?
Yes. Respect.

Nope. She wants presents!

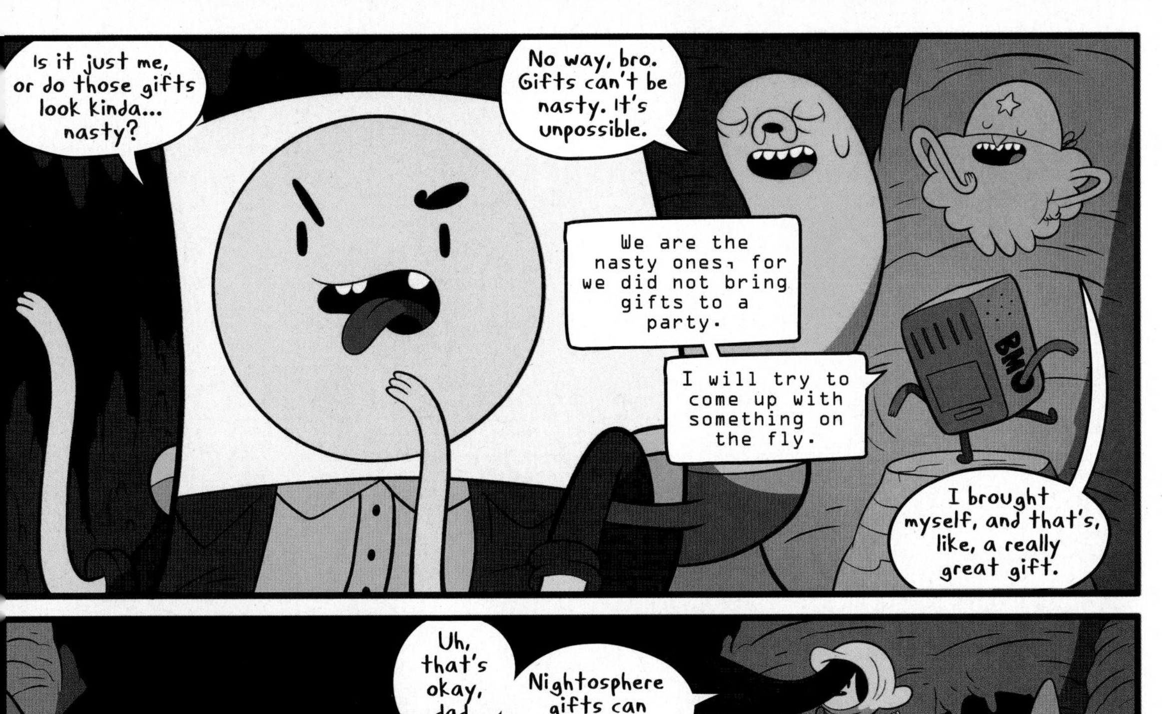
Is it just me, or do those gifts look kinda... nasty?
No way, bro. Gifts can't be nasty. It's unpossible.
We are the nasty ones, for we did not bring gifts to a party.
I will try to come up with something on the fly.
I brought myself, and that's, like, a really great gift.

Uh, that's okay, dad.
Nightosphere gifts can get pretty cray.
I can open those later.
Nonsense! Open your presents.
Your little friends will get a kick out of it.

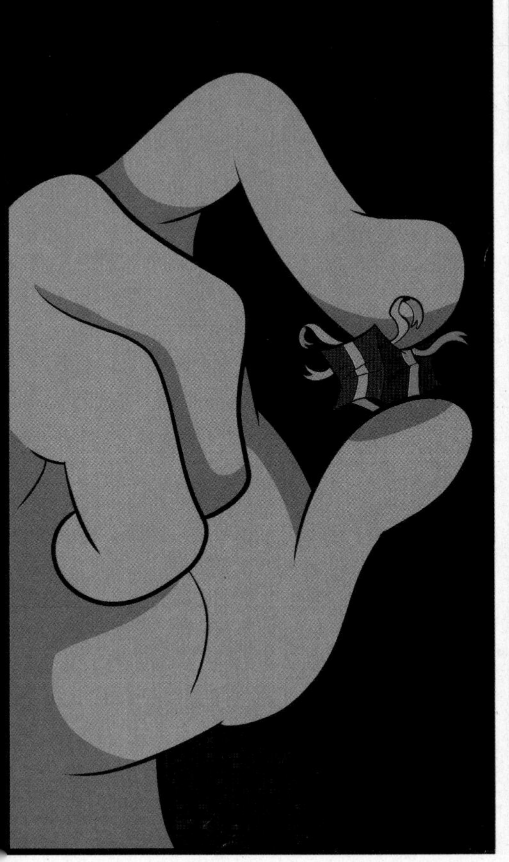

Maybe just a little one.
That's probably harmless enough.

...c'mon...
c'mon...
Dad, what did you do?
Dude, what is that?
I don't know, brotimes, but it's pink.
A whole lotta pink.
I don't like it. It clashes with my lumps.

Dad, it's...
A pony! See? I listen.
You always said you wanted a pony.
His name is Mr. Trots.
You know, it occurs to me that Mr. Trots only eats souls.
Do your friends have souls?
Because that might be a problemo.
Aw! He likes me!
Aw man, he just wants my soul!

Rude!
Get some manners, creepazoid.

DEATHDAY MARC
No! Bad pony! You do not mess up a party by eating souls!
Especially not Jake's soul!
Yeah! My soul is special! Because it's mine!
We do not accept insults from horsies!

Uh, so anybody got a sword? Or an umbrella? Anything?
Because that would be supes handy right now.

SNIFF
SNIFF

Don't worry, Finn. I can handle this one.
Mr. Trots, say hello to my little friend.
I call him... uh...

Mr. Explodey.

Bonni, no! That will only--

BLAM
(BURGLERBLER)!

SPLOOOOT!

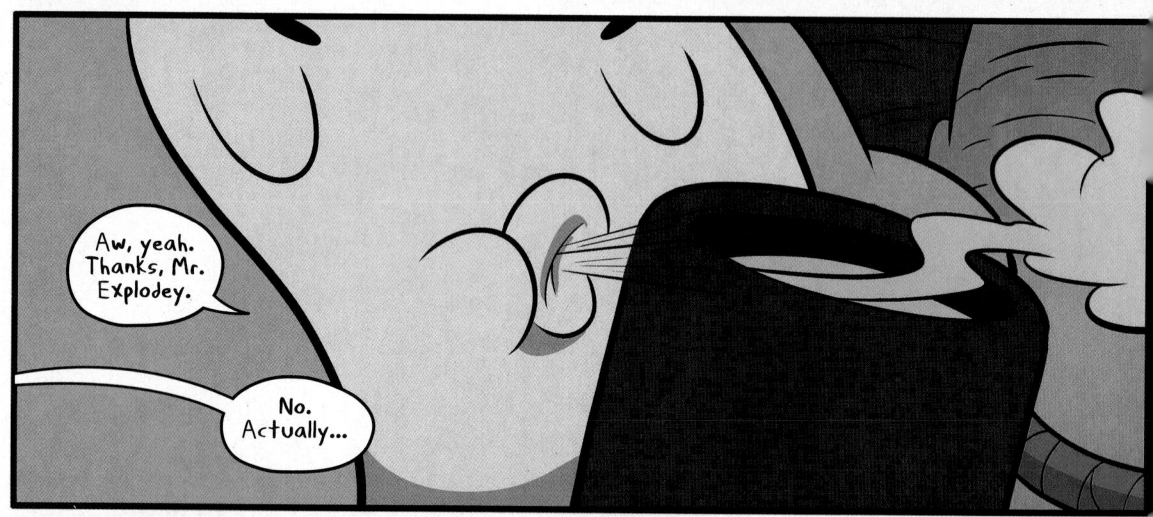
Aw, yeah. Thanks, Mr. Explodey.
No. Actually...

...I was trying to tell you--energy blasts only make Nightosphere creatures bigger and grosser.

If you want to take it down, you're going to need--
Good old-fashioned smasheroony-ing?
Basically.
That was a very nice gift, and now it's all donked up.
And you'd better clean up your mess, young lady!

Jake, it's human torpedo time!
Ready, steady, toasted bready...
Finn-to-face style. How you like it?
DOINK
Man, that is one tough horse.
Time for Plan B.
Also, time to figure out plan B.

Hey, buddy. Just gonna borrow you for a second.
Oh. Hi. My name is Kevin. Wait, you're gonna do what?

Yo, Mr. Trots! Prepare to taste my sword... head...guy. Kevin.

WHOA, HEY THIS IS NOT OKAY!
KA-BOOM!!

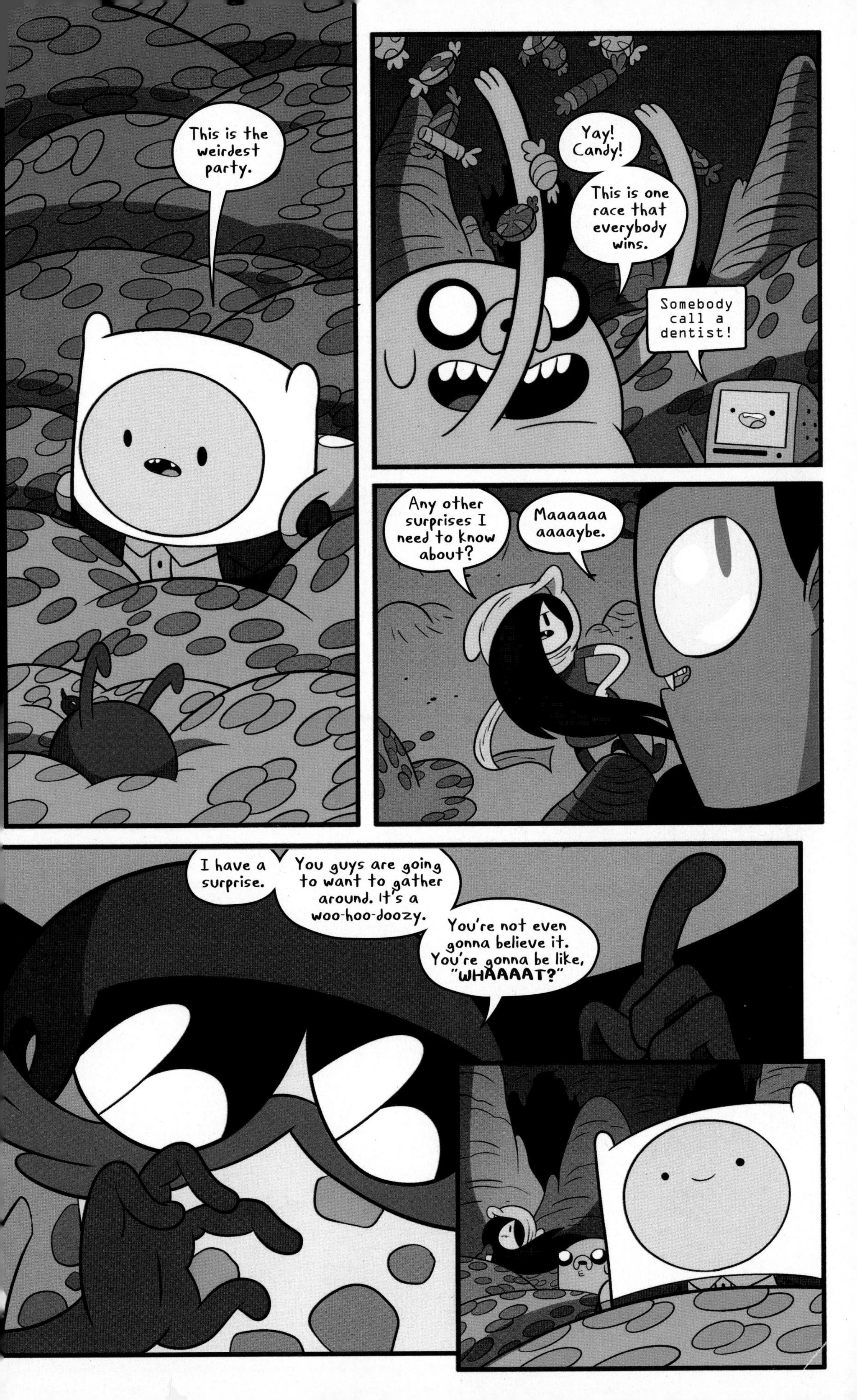
This is the weirdest party.
Yay! Candy!
This is one race that everybody wins.
Somebody call a dentist!
Any other surprises I need to know about?
Maaaaaa aaaaybe.
I have a surprise.
You guys are going to want to gather around. It's a woo-hoo-doozy.
You're not even gonna believe it. You're gonna be like, "**WHAAAAT?**"

I'm actually...

Your old pal Ice King!

We know, dude.
Yeah, we've known the whole time.
BMO IS SHOCKED!

Aw, man! So you also knew that Hunson and I cooked up this biz together?
The race and the rules and the prize and every-thing?
Maybe not everything, but we knew it was you.
The ice Magic was probably the biggest clue.
Yeah, that.
SHOCKED!

Well, fine, then! Here. Have some penguins.
I hope they stink up the place with their fish breath.

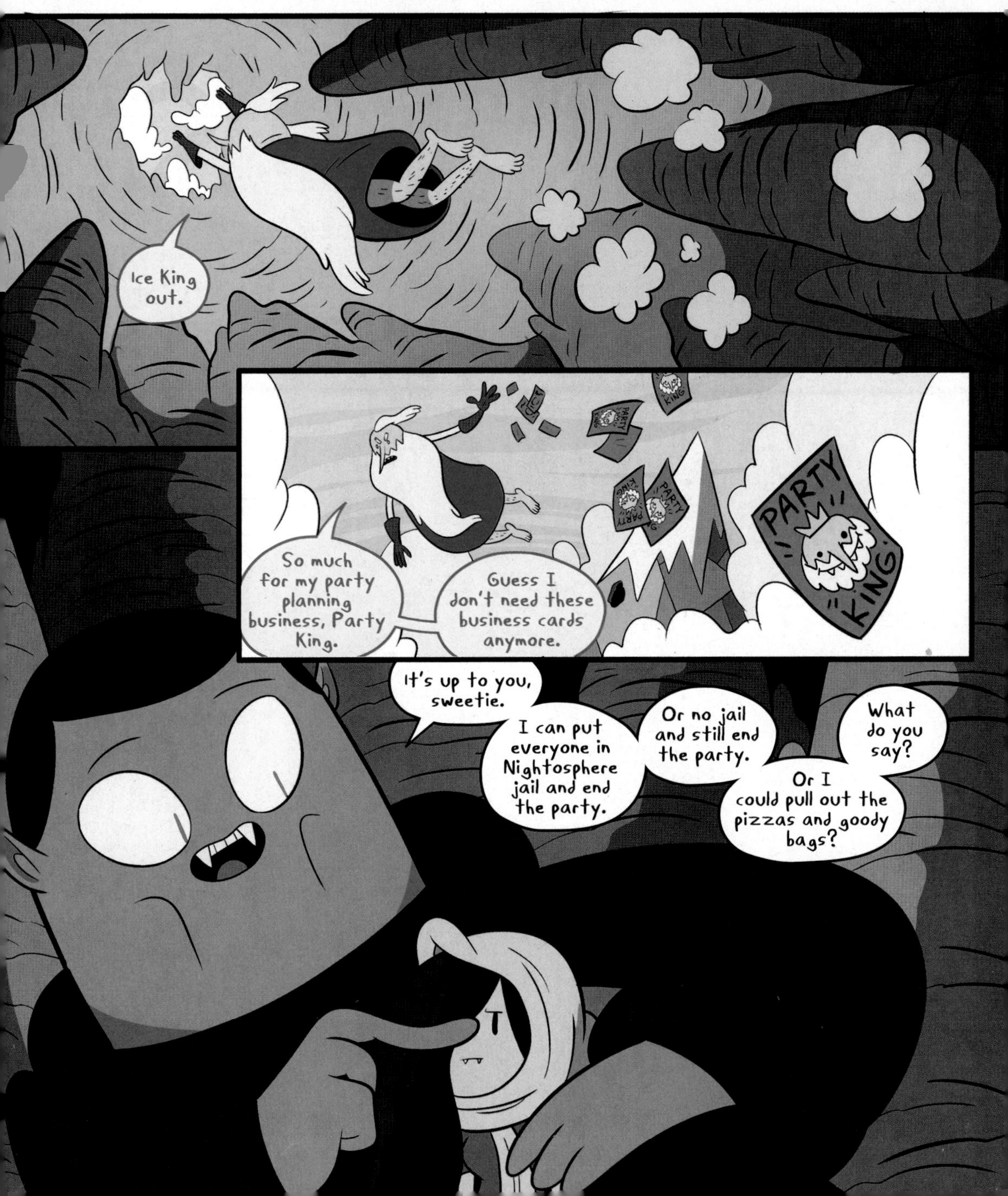
Ice King out.
So much for my party planning business, Party King.
Guess I don't need these business cards anymore.
PARTY KING
It's up to you, sweetie.
I can put everyone in Nightosphere jail and end the party.
Or no jail and still end the party.
Or I could pull out the pizzas and goody bags?
What do you say?

I don't know. What do you guys think?
It's already a pretty good party.
I mean, I got to fight a pony using nothing but Kevin.
The snacks are amazing!
It's not a real party until these lumps win the limbo contest.
You're already in limbo! Mua ha ha ha!
Dad! Come on.
Parties can be fun.
After all, you get to hang out with people who think you're pretty great.
Wait! My gift is ready. Listen, up Marceline:
BMO

Oh, Marcy, it is now your Deathday
We're really happy for you
And glad to be here for you
What kind of friend wouldn't think you're great
Especially on this date
Marcy this was a fun day
Even if you didn't have a say
Happy Deathday!
BMO

Yeah. Okay. We can finish the party. Or whatever.

Hear that? The party's back on!

Hey, guys, I got those hot dog buns--
Whoa. This looks like a great party. Aroooo!

So you're really okay now?
You were right, Bonnibel.
Once you start saying no, it's hard to stop.
It feels kind of okay to say yes instead.
As long as my dad doesn't do anything else stupid.
KNOCK KNOCK KNOCK
Oh, another guest? Whoever could that be?

Look, sweetie! IT'S CLOWNS!
Oh, glob, Dad.

You don't need to be embarrassed. We're having a great time.
Dads are dorks. Everybody knows that.
But clowns are unforgiveable!

Yeah, but they're also fun.
When Stanley showed up in the Candy Kingdom with the race map, I was trying to...
Well, find a way to feel younger. More alive. The race kinda helped.
But putting on a clown nose and dancing like a donkus with my friends helps, too.

Fine. But you have to keep wearing that nose, Bonnibel.
Please refer to me by my clown name, Pinky Bubblebum Quackers.

BMC
Thanks, Dad.

COVER GALLERY

Issue 66 Cover:
Shelli Paroline & Braden Lamb

Issue 66 Subscription Cover:
Michael Bills

Issue 67 Cover:
Shelli Paroline & Braden Lamb

Issue 67 Subscription Cover:
Sean "Cheeks" Galloway

Issue 68 Cover:
Shelli Paroline & Braden Lamb

Issue 68 Subscription Cover:
Matt Smigiel

Issue 69 Cover:
Shelli Paroline & Braden Lamb

Issue 69 Subscription Cover:
Rii Abrego